LOOK AND FIND®

Strawberry Shortcake™

Illustrated by Art Mawhinney
Written by Joanna Spathis

Published by Louis Weber, C.E.O., Publications International, Ltd.
7373 North Cicero Avenue, Lincolnwood, Illinois 60712

Ground Floor, 59 Gloucester Place, London W1U 8JJ

Customer Service: 1-800-595-8484 or customer_service@pilbooks.com

www.pilbooks.com

p i kids is a registered trademark of Publications International, Ltd.

Look and Find is a registered trademark of Publications International, Ltd.,
in the United States and in Canada.

8 7 6 5 4 3 2 1

ISBN-13: 978-1-4127-3932-0
ISBN-10: 1-4127-3932-2

AMERICAN GREETINGS

publications international, ltd.

The Incredible World of DiC

It's a perfect picnic day. Strawberry Shortcake can hardly wait! Before she and her friends head for the beach, she must find her berry favorite red and pink things that she wouldn't dream of leaving behind.

Custard

Jar of jam

Hoodie

Strawberry picnic basket

Pink flip-flops

Everyone has gathered at Angel Cake's house to help bake cakes for their picnic. So many cooks, so many delicious designs! Sift through the flour-filled scene and find these creative creations:

Strawberry's berry tall cake

Huckleberry Pie's purple pie

Orange Blossom's blooming cake

Ginger Snap's super snappy cake

Angel Cake's light and airy cake

Blueberry Muffin's magnificent muffin

Apple Dumplin's cake

Orange Blossom is super-sweet, but also super-shy. Still, she whispered that no one could go on a picnic until they helped her find her fluttering friend, Marmalade. Where could she be? The butterfly garden, of course! Marmalade is gathering flowers for her gift to Orange Blossom. Can you help?

Sparkledrops

Butterflowers

Jinglebells

Oopsidaisies

Lilypops

Golden Melodies

Blueberry Muffin has a great idea: Let's have a parade all the way to the beach! Help gather all the animal friends so they can get marching.

Marmalade

Pupcake

Shoofly Frog

Apple Ducklin'

Vanilla Icing

Custard

Milkshake

Who is already at the beach? Coco Calypso, Rainbow Sherbet, and Seaberry Delight! They're playing party music to welcome Strawberry Shortcake and her friends. Without missing a beat, can you find these fun musical instruments?

Coconutty congas

Beach ball banjo

Tutti-frutti flutey

Mango maracas

Tropical tuba

Banana piano

We dig playing on the beach! There's so much sand, and so many seaberries growing nearby. We build sand sculptures all day long — seaberry sculptures, too! Can you find these creations?

Basket of fruit

Triple Dip Toucan

Strawberry

Gingerbread house

Blueberry Muffin

Lamb

Strawberry Shortcake and her berry best friends had a wonderful time at the beach, but now it's time to head home. Use your finger to trace the way to everybody's house.

Strawberry Shortcake wants to remember everything she did today, so she's writing and drawing in her Remembering Book. Look around her room for these drawings:

Strawberryland is bursting with strawberries, but if you look a little closer you may spot these other favorite juicy fruits!

- ❑ Blueberries
- ❑ Apple
- ❑ Bowl of cherries
- ❑ Pair of pears
- ❑ Orange
- ❑ Watermelon wagon

Oops! Let's help Vanilla Icing tidy up Angel Cake's kitchen. Can you find these goopy goops?

- ❑ Spilled milk
- ❑ Dropped egg
- ❑ Floury flower
- ❑ Sticky paw prints
- ❑ Fallen cake

Who else lives in the butterfly garden? Ladybugs! Go back and see if you can spot twenty of them!

Everyone loves a parade! Can you find these other friends who are all lined up?

- ❑ Butterflies
- ❑ Ants
- ❑ Bumblebees
- ❑ Grasshoppers
- ❑ Birds
- ❑ Ducklings
- ❑ Ladybugs

Can you find these silly dances at the beach party?

❑ The Berry Bounce

❑ The Peppermint Twist

❑ The Chocolate Slide

❑ The Peanut Butter Bump

❑ The Strawberry Swing

❑ The Bubble Up

As you can see, seaberries are super for stacking! Search for these scrumptious seaberry sculptures:

❑ Sea horse
❑ Seagull
❑ Sea turtle
❑ Sea lion
❑ Sea-saw

Uh-oh! Some pages from Strawberry's Remembering Book must have come loose. Go back to her room to find these drawings.

Strawberry's backpack was unbuckled! Go back to the maze to find these things she lost on her way home.

❑ Flip-flop
❑ Seashell
❑ Sand shovel
❑ Beach towel
❑ Water bottle
❑ Comb

Visit www.strawberryshortcake.com to join the Friendship Club and redeem your Strawberry Shortcake Berry Points for "berry" fun stuff!

5

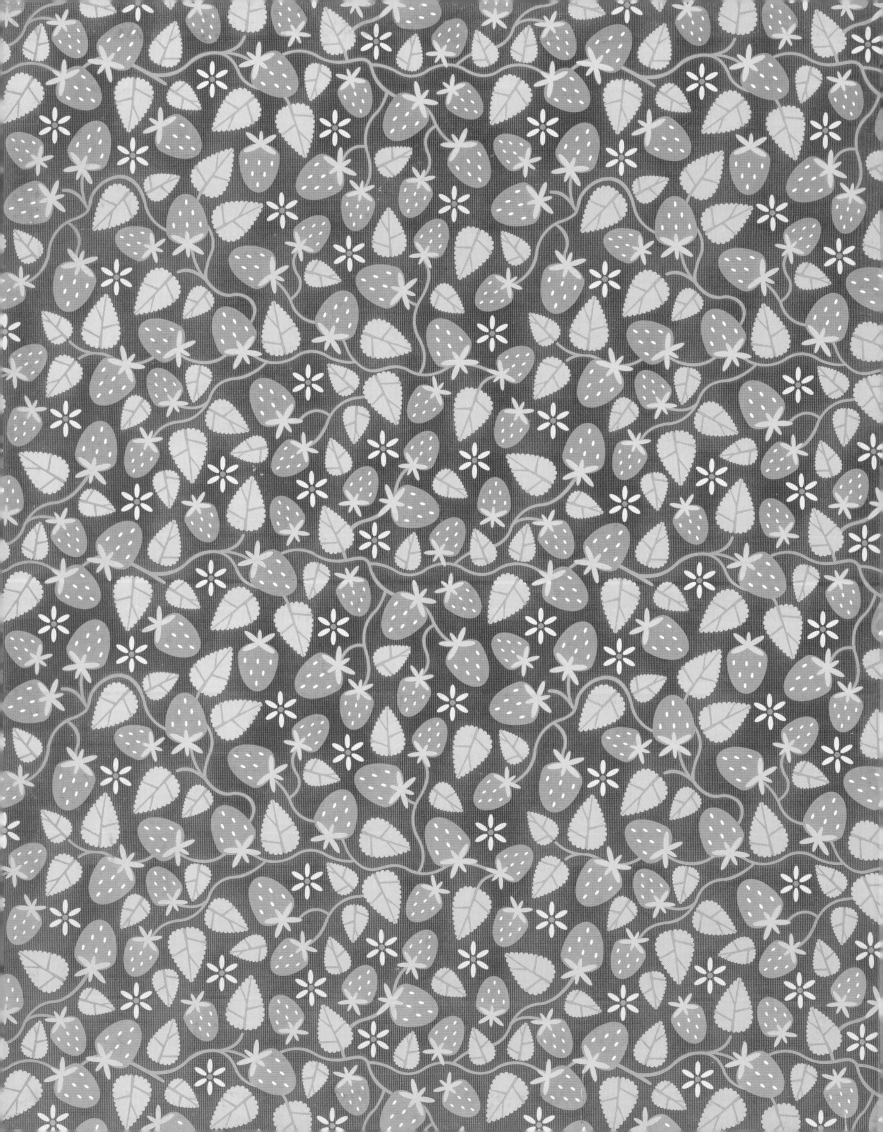